OLIVIA™
and the Perfect Valentine

by Natalie Shaw
illustrated by Shane L. Johnson

Simon Spotlight
New York   London   Toronto   Sydney   New Delhi

Based on the TV series OLIVIA™ as seen on Nickelodeon™

SIMON SPOTLIGHT
An imprint of Simon & Schuster Children's Publishing Division
1230 Avenue of the Americas, New York, New York 10020
OLIVIA™ Ian Falconer Ink Unlimited, Inc. and © 2013 Ian Falconer and Classic Media, LLC. All rights reserved.
All rights reserved, including the right of reproduction in whole or in part in any form.
SIMON SPOTLIGHT and colophon are registered trademarks of Simon & Schuster, Inc.
For information about special discounts for bulk purchases, please contact Simon & Schuster Special Sales
at 1-866-506-1949 or business@simonandschuster.com.
Manufactured in the United States of America 1113 LAK
First Edition 1 2 3 4 5 6 7 8 9 10
ISBN 978-1-4424-8484-9
ISBN 978-1-4424-8485-6 (eBook)

Valentine's Day was one of Olivia's favorite holidays, and it was just around the corner.

"What's so great about Valentine's Day?" asked her little brother Ian.

"Well, it's the one day of the year when *everything* is my favorite color—red!" Olivia replied. "And when there are hearts and lace and pretty things everywhere you look!"

"Yuck," said Ian. "The only kinds of hearts I like are heart-shaped candies."

This year Olivia decided to make her own Valentine's Day cards. She had a stack of red paper, white paper doilies, and lots of crayons.

"See, William," Olivia told her baby brother. "This is how you make paper hearts!"

"First you fold the paper in half," Olivia explained.

"Then you take a crayon and draw half of a heart."

"Next you cut along the crayon line and unfold the paper."

"Ta-da! A perfect heart!"

After cutting out a bunch of hearts for her valentines, Olivia made a list of everyone she wanted to make one for. When she got to Ian's name, she put down her crayon.

"He said he doesn't like hearts, so I don't want to make him a regular valentine," Olivia told William.

Thump! Thump! Olivia could hear Ian kicking the soccer ball around in the backyard.

"That's it!" Olivia said. Ian loves soccer so she could make the perfect valentine
for him by decorating a heart with soccer balls!
It looked so great that she decided to make perfect valentines for everyone. They
would all be different because everyone liked different things, but they would all
have one thing in common: they would be red!

Olivia made valentines for Mother, Father, Grandmother, and William, too. But there were still more names on her list. She decided to take a little break and go outside.

"Hmm," Olivia wondered aloud. "I have the feeling I'm forgetting someone. Who else needs a perfect valentine?"

"Me!" said a voice. It was Olivia's friend Francine.
Francine's name was already on Olivia's list. Olivia invited her to come inside
and make valentines with her.

Olivia made a valentine for Francine.

And Francine made one for Olivia.

They promised not to peek at each other's cards so they would be a surprise on Valentine's Day.

Then they both made valentines for Daisy, Harold, and Julian.

But Olivia still had the feeling she was forgetting someone.

"Mrs. Hoggenmuller!" Francine said.

But Mrs. Hoggenmuller was already on Olivia's list.

Olivia made a heart for her teacher, and decorated it with a picture of her pet turkey, chalk, and a chalkboard eraser.

Then she made one for the postman, and another for Firefighter Fred.

After that, Olivia couldn't think of anyone else to make a card for, and all the names on her list were checked off.

"Well, I guess that's it!" Olivia said.

"See you tomorrow," Francine replied. "I mean, see you on Valentine's Day!"

In Mrs. Hoggenmuller's class the next day, Olivia passed out her valentines and received a bunch in return. Francine gave her a valentine with red stripes on it. "I love it!" said Olivia. "It matches my favorite shirt!"

"And I love the ribbons on my valentine," said Francine. "They match my favorite ribbons!"

Julian looked at his card and smiled. "How'd you know that I love music?" he asked Olivia.

"And that I love daisies?" asked Daisy.

"And that I love frogs?" asked Harold.

"Because you're my friends!" replied Olivia. "Happy Valentine's Day, everyone!"

After school Olivia walked around the neighborhood with her mom and passed out more valentines.

"Thank you, Olivia!" said Firefighter Fred.
"It's perfect!" said the postman. "How did you guess that I collect stamps?"

That night at dinner Olivia gave cards to everyone in her family, too.

"Thanks, Olivia!" Ian smiled. "I love soccer!"

But she still felt like she was forgetting someone.

And then, just before bedtime, it hit her . . . she forgot all about Perry and Edwin!
"They're part of the family, too!" Olivia exclaimed. "How could I forget to make them perfect valentines?"
"Don't worry, Olivia," Dad said. "They know you love them. Now off to bed!"

"But I know what I can make them," Olivia explained. "I can put dog bones on Perry's card, and cat treats on Edwin's card . . ."

"I have an idea, Olivia," Mom replied. "Why don't you tell them how much you love them? And maybe give them some treats too?"

Olivia thought about it and decided her mom was right. There probably was nothing better for her pets!